Family

cowboy boot

Grandma Thora

stuffed bunny

alarm clock

lollipop

suspenders

handkerchief

footstool

doll carriage

Grandpa Dave

pudding

toothpaste

rubber duckie

baby bottle

D.W.

toothbrush

Baby Kate

pacifier

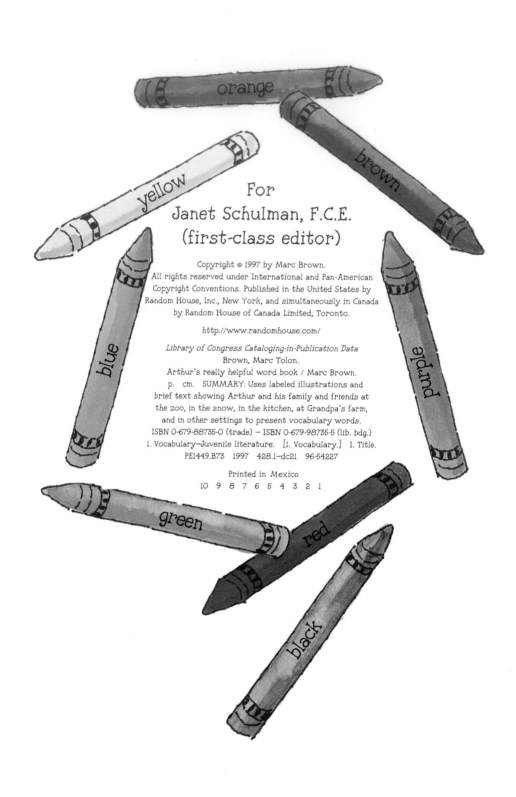

For
Janet Schulman, F.C.E.
(first-class editor)

Copyright © 1997 by Marc Brown.
All rights reserved under International and Pan-American
Copyright Conventions. Published in the United States by
Random House, Inc., New York, and simultaneously in Canada
by Random House of Canada Limited, Toronto.

http://www.randomhouse.com/

Library of Congress Cataloging-in-Publication Data
Brown, Marc Tolon.
Arthur's really helpful word book / Marc Brown.
p.   cm.   SUMMARY: Uses labeled illustrations and
brief text showing Arthur and his family and friends at
the zoo, in the snow, in the kitchen, at Grandpa's farm,
and in other settings to present vocabulary words.
ISBN 0-679-88735-0 (trade) — ISBN 0-679-98735-5 (lib. bdg.)
1. Vocabulary–Juvenile literature.   [1. Vocabulary.]   1. Title.
PE1449.B73   1997   428.1—dc21   96-54227

Printed in Mexico
10 9 8 7 6 5 4 3 2 1

scissors

hairbrush

lizard

 pen

T-shirt

belt

birthday cake

party hat

slippers

baby powder

pajamas

telephone

spaghetti

anchor

drum

recorder

undershirt

balloon

Random House New York

beads

present

ARTHUR'S REALLY HELPFUL
Word Book
MARC BROWN

fireplace

roof

shutters

highchair

paintbrush

awning

light switch

light bulb

towel

soap dish

shower curtain

shampoo

door

mirror

faucet

toilet

tub

sink

At Arthur's House

Saturday is clean-up day and everyone is busy. What are some of the things you can do to help around your house?

staircase

piano

chair

telephone

chest

table

circuit breaker

steps

tools

dirty clothes

vise

workbench

oil can

hot water heater

paint cans

matches

ironing board

iron

needle & thread

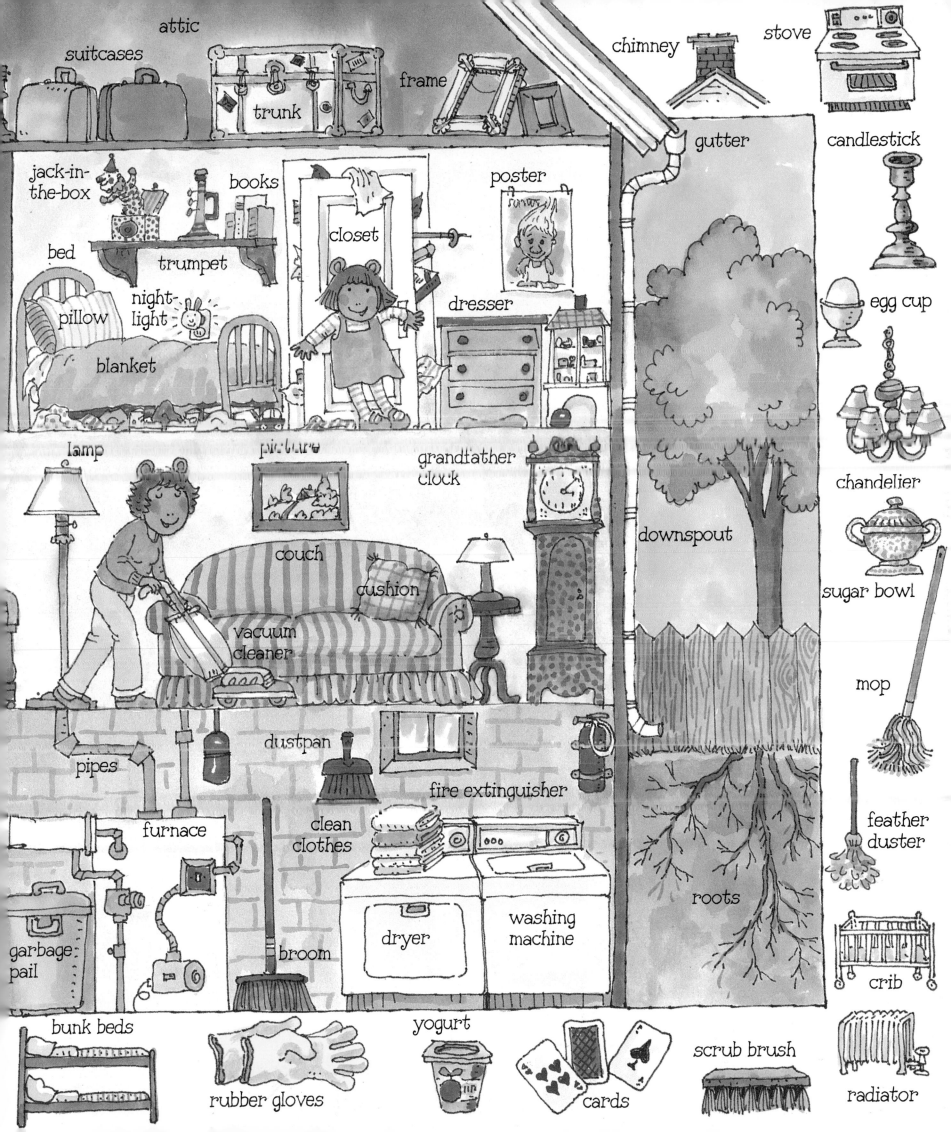

attic

suitcases

trunk

frame

chimney

stove

gutter

candlestick

jack-in-the-box

books

poster

egg cup

bed

closet

trumpet

pillow

night-light

dresser

chandelier

blanket

lamp

picture

grandfather clock

downspout

sugar bowl

couch

cushion

mop

vacuum cleaner

dustpan

pipes

fire extinguisher

roots

feather duster

furnace

clean clothes

garbage pail

broom

dryer

washing machine

crib

bunk beds

rubber gloves

yogurt

cards

scrub brush

radiator

deer

shark

elephant

crocodile

lion

At the Zoo

Watching the sea lions is always fun, but today there is some real monkey business going on at the zoo. All of the monkeys have escaped. Can you help the zookeeper find them?

zebra

giraffe

ticket booth

bird

turnstile

zookeeper

ostrich

stroller

panda

camel

dolphin

tiger

penguin

buffalo

leopard

hippopotamus

snake

hoop

parrots

fish

bucket

ball

sea lion

cardinal

balloons

turtle

gorilla

ICE CREAM

dog

anteater

polar bear

fox

peacock

At School with D.W.

Everyone is very busy at school today, including the class gerbil. He likes stories too!

A armadillo
B beehive
C clown
D dolphin
E ear

Z zipper
Y yarn
X x-ray
W whale
V violin
U unicorn
T tea kettle
S skateboard

hat
lunchbox
plant
cactus
calendar
MAY
chalkboard
ELIZA TOJON
toy refrigerator
coat rack
mittens
cage
boots
puppet
top hat
toy stove
pot
toy sink
easel
high heels
crown
cowboy hat
paintbrush

Counting

From 1 to 10 – can you count these city things?

2 two fire stations

3 three apartment buildings

4 four statues

5 five trees

6 six fire hydrants

7 seven stop signs

8 eight mailboxes

9 nine traffic lights

1 one skyscraper

10 ten trash cans

Opposites

Do you know any others? Yes? No?

up   down   hot   cold   over   under

full   empty   asleep   awake   high   low

slow   fast   happy   sad   on   off

big   little   sweet   sour   young   old

The Three Little Pigs

Little Red Riding Hood

Grandma

The Big Bad Wolf

castle

sword

dragon

princess

Jack and the beanstalk

knight in armor

GREAT STORIES

Storyland

Arthur loves to read stories.
He also likes to make up his own.
Would you like to make up a story?

giant

Goldilocks

The Three Bears

Cinderella

prince

planet

antennae

alien

spacesuit

spaceship

gingerbread house

Hansel and Gretel

witch

sails

flag

Humpty Dumpty

ship

pirate

cannons

treasure chest

Tinker Bell

Peter Pan

At the Supermarket

Arthur has to do some shopping. Can you help him find everything on his list?

juice

peaches

ice cream

banana

raspberries

pear

lime

eggplant

peas

lettuce

toilet paper

MEAT

chicken

butcher

steaks

sausages

HOUSEHOLD

paper towels

BAKERY

rolls

bread

cakes

cereal
pineapple
eggs
paper towels
bread

shopping cart

apples

soap

flour

jam

celery

cucumber

batteries

tissues

lemon

cantaloupe

dish soap

tuna fish

kiwi

garlic

beet

mustard

orange

soda

SPECIAL

bagels

pineapples

CEREAL

muffins

DAIRY

butter

yogurt

cheese

soup

pie

milk

eggs

Swiss cheese

sauce

spaghetti

watermelon

pepper

gloves

snowball

cap

hockey stick

hockey puck

valentine

thermometer

icicles

snowflakes

snow shovel

bird feeder

fire hydrant

pipe

scarf

snowman

snowsuit

boots

mitten

Winter

It's a snowy day, and
the whole world is covered in white.
But there are some bright red things that stand out.
How many can you find?

blue jay

skis

poles

ice skates

goggles

earmuffs

toboggan

birdbath

gate

toad

mailbox

tricycle

roller skates

eggs

nest

triangle

square

chimney

roof

diamond

circle

bone

butterfly

string

rain hat

helmet

raincoat

galoshes

bicycle

training wheels

umbrella

tulip

crocus

robin

daffodil

Spring

It is a beautiful day for flying kites and having fun! These kites are all different shapes. What shapes do you see?

puddle

snail

rake

hose

trowel

seeds

flowerpot

watering can

fan

ice cream truck

ice cream cone

ice cream pop

lobster

sandals

sunblock

Summer

A picnic at the beach is delicious on a hot summer day. The ants think so too. How many ants came to Arthur's picnic?

lighthouse

cliff

sailboat

motorboat

buoy

wave

dune

beach ball

beach bag

bathing suit

picnic basket

chips

shell

beach blanket

cup

sandwich

plate

gull

shovel

pail

sand castle

ants

starfish

lawnmower

sunglasses

beach umbrella

crab

pitcher

dandelion

seeds

Wampanoag Indians*

Pilgrim

turkey

moth

squirrel

acorn

wheelbarrow

branches

knife

window

leaves

tree

bush

happy

sad

surprised

pumpkin

jack-o'-lanterns

sweater

rake

Fall

D.W. is helping Arthur rake leaves.
Dad is getting ready for Halloween.
What kinds of faces did he carve?

*The Wampanoags were the Native Americans who attended the Pilgrims' first Thanksgiving.

football

gourds

witch

bat

ghost

cornstalks

mask

bull

cherries

calf

goose

tomato

At Grandpa Dave's Farm

Arthur is learning how to milk a cow. The cow has something to say about that: Moooooooo! What do some of the other animals say?

wheat

hoe

milk can

Oink-oink

Mooooooooo

pig

pigsty

cow

fly

tail

cowbell

Meow-meow

udder

pail

cat

stool

mouse

horseshoe

hay wagon

onions

watch

medicine

jellybeans

scale

shoes

French fries

television

popcorn

candy

dress

perfume

art supplies

BANK
ATM

CINEMA

NOW PLAYING
BIONIC BUNNY ON MARS   G
PRETTY PONY COME HOME   G

Ice Cream Shop

TICKET BOOTH

escalator

OUT

IN

walkie-talkie

security guard

At the Shopping Mall

Arthur and D.W. agreed on a birthday present for their mom. But they can't agree on what movie to see. What movie do you think they should see?

pretzel

skirt

blouse

hair dryer

radio

soap

dice

video camera

basket

magazine

armchair

toaster

jeans

diamond ring

Bookstore

Toy Store

sundae

Jewelry

marionette

present

bracelet

necklace   rings

dollhouse

robot

greeting card

bathrobe

pay telephone

fountain

bath brush

litter can

shopping bag

tennis racket

shorts

sled

newspaper

underwear

milkshake

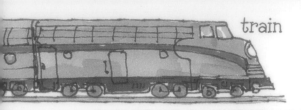 train

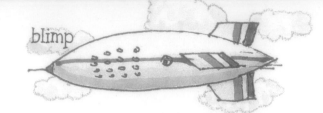 blimp

 submarine

Things That Go

What's your favorite way to get from here to there?

Screech!

bicycle

delivery van

Renita's Flowers

Honk! Honk!

RELIABLE MOVERS

moving truck

Honk! Honk!

taxi

Beep! Beep!
Beep! Beep!

TAXI

Whee-eeee! Whee-eee!

police car

POLICE

Piccadilly Circu

racing car

bulldozer

jeep

oil tank truck

swimming pool

star

lantern

duffel bag

compass

cooler

thermos

sleeping bag

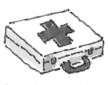
first-aid kit

bug repellent

firewood

Backyard Camping

Telling spooky stories around the campfire can make you imagine all sorts of strange things. What do you see in the clouds?

clouds

smoke

log

marshmallows

water bottle

fire

flashlight

raisins

fishing pole

fish

fishing net

Ping-Pong paddle

Ping-Pong ball

tadpole

hammock

tennis ball

moth

dragonfly

fly

fly swatter

owl

moon

sky

lightning bugs

fern

tent

birdhouse

hot dog

binoculars

snail

blanket

pillow

magnifying glass

raccoon

mushroom

worm

skunk

What's Inside?

Baby Kate has turned everything upside down. What a mess! Can you help Arthur and D.W. put everything back where it belongs?

toolbox

change purse
tissues
pen
keys
lipstick
comb
chewing gum
notebook

blocks
truck
teddy bear
doll
pull toy
yo-yo

lunchbox

screws
screwdriver
pliers
nails
hammer
drill
tape measure

pocketbook

cookie
carrot sticks
juice
sandwich
apple
napkin

toy chest

When Arthur Grows Up...
Here are some of the things he might be.

astronaut

fire fighter

police officer

cowboy

soldier

doctor

artist

rock star

teacher

chef

jester

construction worker

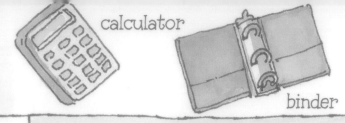 calculator

 marker

 envelope

 stamp

 hole puncher

binder

Mom at Work

Mom is an accountant. D.W. loves to visit her office. There are so many interesting things there, including a mouse that doesn't eat cheese. Can you find it?

cup

bulletin board

lamp

pictures

briefcase

computer

telephone

important letters

drawer

desk

files

wastebasket

stapler

carpeting

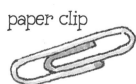 paper clip

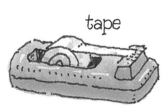 tape

 rubber bands

 pencil sharpener

 pushpin

 eraser

 thumbtack

wooden spoon

cookie cutters

birthday candles

measuring spoons

tongs

salt

pepper

timer

Dad at Work

Arthur's dad is a caterer. Sometimes Arthur helps him clean up.
He is very good at licking the spoons.

coffee

cooking oil

magnets

cupboard

microwave oven

dish soap

freezer

refrigerator

cake

sink

jam

pot

blender

mixing bowl

whisk

spatula

pastry bag

pan

flour

rice

sugar

cake flour

dishwasher

colander

tray

rolling pin

potholder

sponge

measuring cup

electric mixer

bench

dandelion

stream

bridge

swan

clover

pigeon

top

sweatshirt

rings

jungle gym

litter basket

At the Playground

D.W. is playing hide-and-seek and she is "it." Can you help her find Arthur, Muffy, Francine, and Binky? (Their pictures are on the last two pages.)

swings

...ready or not, here I come!

sandbox

sand

pail

grass

seesaw

pussywillow

jacks

spider

bandage

whistle

ladybug

slide

lunchbox

jump rope

lamppost

bouncing ball

bell

basketball

caterpillar

water lily

basketball hoop

ladder

playhouse

squirrel

merry-go-round

pogo stick

sidewalk

hopscotch game

sun

sand toys

trike

marbles

buttons

bottle caps

stamps

Diplodocus

Cetiosaurus

Collections

Buster has quite a collection of toy dinosaurs! People can collect all sorts of things. Do you have a collection?

dolls

marbles

pencils

caps

rocks

postcards

feathers

toy cars

coins

Stegosaurus

Triceratops

Allosaurus

shells

Tyrannosaurus rex

action figures

baseball cards

teddy bears

ballet slippers

Arthur's

star

tooth

Prunella

Binky Barnes

moon

Arthur

guitar

flippers

bubble gum

braids

potato chips

tic-tac-toe

tambourine

Buster

Muffy